The Witch's Birthday Present

Written and illustrated by

Carolyn Dinan

Hamish Hamilton
London

Ada Witch woke up in a specially bad
mood.

"It's my birthday today," she said. "I
bet no one's remembered. They never do.
What's the good of having a birthday if you
don't get any presents?"

But at the end of her bed was a big pink
envelope.

"A letter," said Ada. "For me!"

5

Ada opened the letter.

"It's from my sister, Winnie," she cried. "And she's sending me a pet. I've always wanted a cat. How ever did she know?"

Dear Ada
Happy Birthday!
I am sending you a
PRESENT!
A dear little pet to
keep you company.
Love,
Winnie xxxx
P.S. He's called Paws.
P.P.S. Look out of your
window.

Ada looked out of the window. She could see a basket flying through the sky towards her.

"It's my cat," she shrieked. "Here it comes!"

The basket sailed through the window and landed on the table.

Ada untied the string and lifted the lid.

"Out you come, Kitty," cooed Ada. "Who's a pretty cat then?"

But he wasn't a cat at all.

Ada rang Winnie right away.

"Happy Birthday, dear," said Winnie.

"I'm not a bit happy," said Ada. "What am I supposed to do with this dog?"

"Well . . . look after him," replied Winnie in surprise. "Feed him and train him and take him for lovely long walks."

"But what about ME?" demanded Ada.
"What do I get out of it?"

"He'll be a real friend. You won't be
lonely with him around," said Winnie.

"I don't want a friend," said Ada.
"Friends are hard work. I want a cat.
C.A.T. To help with my spells. A dog is no
use at all."

But Ada was wrong. Paws was very useful.

She didn't need an alarm clock any more because he woke her up every morning, licking her face with his big pink tongue.

And every afternoon he took her for long healthy walks.

The schoolchildren, who had shouted
rude words and made faces through her
window, now came to play in the garden
with Paws.

And in the evening Paws fetched her
slippers and curled up in front of the fire
with her.

But it was no good. Ada was determined.

"What I want is a little cat. A dog is
nothing but trouble."

Then Ada had an idea.

"Why didn't I think of it before?" she cried. She got out her Spell Book and a big saucepan.

PLIP PLOP POP SPLAT! bubbled the mixture.

"I'll show Winnie," said Ada as she stirred away. "I'm going to get a little cat of my own at last instead of that silly dog."

Ada poured the mixture into a bowl and
let it cool.

"Now, Paws," she beamed. "Eat up, like
a good dog."

And Paws gobbled it all up and licked the
bowl clean.

"Rruff," he barked in astonishment.
"Rruff . . . rreowww . . . meeowwwww!"

Ada glared at Paws. "You greedy
creature. You shouldn't have eaten all of
the spell," she said. "I didn't want you to
be *that* little. What I need is a BIG cat; a
little cat is no use at all."

Ada got out her Spell Book again.

"This time," she said, "I'll get it right."

GURGLE GLOOGLE GLOP spat the mixture.

"Nearly done," said Ada. "I'll put a few drops in this lid for you . . . that's right, Paws, you're going to turn into a lovely big cat . . . a Big Cat? Oh no! Stop!"

But it was too late.

There stood the biggest lion Ada had ever seen. He opened his great mouth showing sharp white teeth.

"RRRRRAAAGGGGGHHHHHH," roared the lion.

"Eeek," said Ada.

Ada shut herself in her bedroom.

"I've had quite enough for today," she sighed. "I'm going to sleep."

Next morning, the lion woke her with a big lick.

"Oh, my warts and whiskers," wailed Ada. "I thought you were trying to eat me."

She tottered downstairs to put the kettle on. The lion drank up all the tea, and ate up all Ada's food.

Then he lay across the doorway in the bright sunshine and closed his eyes.

"At least I don't have to take you out for a walk," said Ada. "I can stay in all day."

But it was dusty and dark and cold indoors.

The children arrived in the garden after
school.

"Paws!" they shouted. "Where are you?"

"RrrraagGGGHHH!" roared the lion
happily, and waved a friendly paw.

"Hee-hee," cackled Ada. "They're all
running away. Good riddance."

But the garden seemed very silent and
lonely after they had gone.

That evening, Paws dozed in front of the
fire.

"Move over, you lazy lump!" said Ada
rudely.

The lion opened his eyes and yawned
slowly.

Ada had never seen so many big fierce
teeth.

"I've gone right off cats," she shrieked in
alarm. "And I certainly don't want a lion.
What I want is a dog. D.O.G. To keep me
company. To be a friend. A lion is no use at
all."

Ada got out her Spell Book again.

"This time," she said, "nothing can go wrong."

BUBBLE PLUBBLE GLUBBLE BANG!

Ada spooned the Spell into a big bowl.

"Good boy, Paws," she said. "Dinner's ready."

The lion looked at Ada and licked his lips.

"Come on," said Ada nervously. "Don't be silly."

She dipped the spoon in the mixture and took a large slurp.

"I'll just make sure it's cool enough . . . wuff . . ."

. . . woof . . . WOOF . . . **WOOF!**

Ada and Paws went to stay with Winnie
until the spell wore off. Winnie was very
pleased to see them once she had got over
the shock.

But she wouldn't undo the spell.

"It's time you learnt a lesson, Ada dear,"
she said.

At last, one fine morning, they woke up and found they were their old selves again.

Well, not quite.

"I don't know what's got into me," said Ada, as she patted Paws on the head. "I knew I'd be glad to see me again but I never thought I'd be so glad to see you."

"Woof," panted Paws eagerly. "Miaoww . . . ? Rrraghh . . . ? WOOF!"

And he put his nose on Ada's lap and gave her a big wet lick.

When Ada got home she put her Spell Book away in the cupboard and locked the door.

And she didn't make another spell for a very long time.